PiXies
VS
FAiRiES

Published in 2023 by Welbeck Flame
An imprint of Welbeck Children's Limited,
part of Welbeck Publishing Group.
Offices in: London - 20 Mortimer Street, London W1T 3JW &
Sydney - Level 17, 207 Kent St, Sydney NSW 2000 Australia
www.welbeckpublishing.com

Design and layout © Welbeck Children's Limited 2022
Text copyright © Tibor Jones
Illustrations copyright © Katy Halford, 2023

Tibor Jones and Katy Halford have asserted their moral right
to be identified as the Author and Illustrator of this Work in accordance
with the Copyright Designs and Patents Act 1988.

A CIP catalogue record for this book is available from the British Library.

ISBN: 978 1 80130 089 6

Printed and bound by CPI Group (UK)

10 9 8 7 6 5 4 3 2 1

Disclaimer: Any names, characters, trademarks, service marks and
trade names detailed in this book is the property of their respective
owners and are used solely for identification and reference purposes.
This book is a publication of Welbeck Children's Limited, part of
Welbeck Publishing Group and has not been licensed, approved,
sponsored or endorsed by any person or entity.

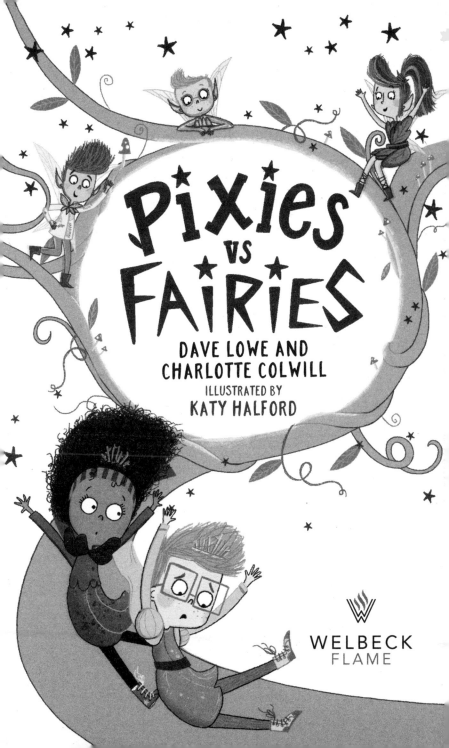

Pixies vs Fairies

DAVE LOWE AND CHARLOTTE COLWILL

ILLUSTRATED BY
KATY HALFORD

WELBECK
FLAME

PROLOGUE

I'm sure you've heard of fairies.
You've probably heard of pixies too.
But maybe you thought they only
existed in stories. You might imagine fairies
with colourful wings, sitting on toadstools,
eating tiny cupcakes and living in harmony.
That's what I thought, too. Until I found
myself on an adventure and discovered
that everything we've been told about
fairies – and pixies – is completely wrong!

Chapter ONE

I was at the foot of a huge mountain, staring up at the icy peak and wondering just how to get there.

Well, I was actually in the living room of our new place, staring up at the pyramid of still-unopened cardboard boxes that the removal men had left there. But in my imagination, it was a mountain. My little brother Oscar was next to me, holding the flag that I'd made for my mission – the flag which I'd soon be planting at the very top.

I was halfway up when Dad ducked his shiny, bald head in from the kitchen, and gasped. 'Alice – careful!'

'But I'm near the top of the mountain, Dad,' I said.

'And I'm worried you'll slip on the ice and plummet,' he said. 'Rescue helicopter incoming!'

He dashed over, making a helicopter sound – **WOKKA-WOKKA WOKKA** – lifted me off and placed me on the carpet next to my brother.

'Oscar,' Dad added. 'Flags are for waving, not for eating, please!'

BITS + BOBS

BOOKS

SPARE BEDDING

Dad went back to the kitchen to finish cooking and, just like that, my attempt to reach the peak of Mount Cardboard was over.

When Mum and Dad told me that we were moving to a quiet village, not far from the sea, but a really long way from all my friends, I was miserable. I didn't know *anyone* here – and there was nothing exciting to do.

Our new house is an old cottage with a roof made from straw. Because of the story of the three little pigs, I was a bit nervous about the whole 'straw' thing, but Dad said it was super-strong and not to worry – no amount of huffing or puffing would blow it down.

Because Dad had ruined my climbing expedition, I found the box that he'd marked

'Alice's Adventure Equipment', pulled out my binoculars and looked out of the window.

Our new garden is long and dotted with a few big trees and patches of tall white-and-red flowers. There's a tiny stream at the end and, beyond that, huge fields surrounded by hedgerows and more trees. It's true what Mum says – that the sky seems much bigger and bluer here. The scenery's beautiful too, just as she said it would be. But it just seemed... too quiet. What adventures could possibly happen here?

I sighed. I was stuck. It was just me, lots and lots of trees, my unadventurous parents, and my super-dribbly baby brother – who had put down the flag but was now chewing his toy giraffe. Oscar is only one and a half and his hobbies are chewing things, smearing food all over his face, and following me around all the time.

Dad called, 'Dinner's ready!' so I scooped Oscar up and carried him into the kitchen. He is a heavy lump but luckily I'm strong – like all adventurers. Dad, in his 'World's Greatest Chef' apron, was serving up bowls of macaroni cheese with peas on the side. This is my all-time favourite meal, so I could tell that he was trying to cheer me up about the move.

Dad wears glasses and has a head that's as smooth as a pebble. He bakes delicious cakes, does funny voices and makes up songs about ordinary things like brushing our teeth and cleaning our bedroom, which makes those things more fun – a bit, at least. Dad's job is looking after me and Oscar and he is mostly great at it. He was singing one of his songs as he put our plates in front of us, accompanied by a wiggly dance.

'Whose peas are these? Alice's peas! And what about these? Oscar's peas! And look at this – macaroni cheese! Do I want it in my tum? Mmm. Yes, please!' We giggled, then heard the front door unlock and swing open. 'Who's at the door?!' Dad sang. 'It's Mummy – for sure!'

Oscar bopped up and down as Mum

appeared in the kitchen doorway in her purple work scrubs. Mum is super-tall and has fabulous curly hair, which she kindly passed on to me. She loves cups of tea, reading books and fixing things like clothes and vases (I sometimes break things while on adventures). She's a surgeon, which means her job is to help fix people too.

Mum came over and kissed Oscar on the one tiny patch of his face that didn't have macaroni cheese on it. He clapped delightedly. Then she kissed me on my forehead. I smiled – but only a bit. Because even seeing Mum *and* eating my favourite food couldn't make up for the fact that we'd moved to the middle of nowhere.

'Give it a chance, pal,' said Dad gently.

'There's plenty of animals around here — ones that you won't see in London.'

'Dragons?' I said.

'Well, no but...'

'Monkeys? Hippos? Penguins?'

'No, but — you know: cows, sheep, chickens...'

'There's absolutely nothing to do here,' I said, 'and I don't know *anyone*. It's no fun, going on adventures by yourself.'

'You'll meet new people,' said Mum, reaching over to ruffle my hair. 'And you *will* find adventure. I just know it.'

Oscar, feeling left out of the conversation, blew a big raspberry.

'Hang on a sec,' said Dad, looking out of the window into our back garden. 'There's a person in shorts down there. He looks about your size, Alice!'

I shovelled a few more spoonfuls of macaroni into my mouth, rushed to the back door and peered through my binoculars. I saw trees, trees, sky, more trees, another tree... and then... **WHAT WAS THAT?** I whipped back and focused my gaze on the face of a boy, looking right back at me. I lowered the binoculars and could see him standing on the other side of the fence, not very far away, halfway down the garden. I inspected him with my binoculars again. He had messy red hair, glasses – and dirty knees, which were surely the sign of an adventurer. Maybe, just maybe, this boy could be my new friend.

I pulled on my shoes and raced out into the back garden.

'Don't go too far, Alice!' Mum called after

me. 'It's bath night. And even adventurers need to wash their hair sometimes.'

CHAPTER TWO

'Hello!' I called out.

The boy looked behind him as if I was speaking to someone else.

'Hello,' he said eventually, and gave me a tiny wave.

I bounded down the garden and peered at him over the low fence. A fluffy black cat danced around his feet in a figure of eight.

'I'm Alice!' I said breathlessly. 'I'm eight years and one month old and we've just moved here!'

He looked down at his feet and fidgeted with the bottom of his yellow T-shirt.

'I'm Max,' he mumbled. 'I'm seven and...' He counted slowly on his fingers. '...nine months.'

'Do you live here?' I asked.

He nodded. 'With my grandma – and Lola.'

'Lola?' I said, really hoping that he had an older sister who might be better suited for adventures than *he* was. But he pointed at the cat. 'Oh,' I said. To fill the silence, I added, 'Do you like it here? It's really quiet, don't you think?'

He shrugged. He seemed about as good at conversations as my brother (but at least he wasn't chewing random objects, I suppose). 'There are lots of *trees*, though,' he said. 'I like trees.'

'Well, you're definitely in the right place,' I said, with a sigh. Then, without much optimism, I asked, 'Do you ever go on any adventures?'

'Adventures?' Max said, looking behind him and biting his thumb. 'Not really.'

'So what do you do, then? For fun? Look at trees?'

He shrugged. 'I do magic,' he said, and pulled a tatty pack of cards out of his shorts pocket and shuffled them. He was surprisingly good at shuffling. And with the cards in his hands, his face changed – he was more confident, somehow.

'Pick a card,' he said, fanning the deck out and presenting it to me. 'Look at it, put it back, and don't tell me what it is.'

I chose a card, glanced at it – the King of Diamonds – and put it back.

'Now spin round three times,' he said, 'while thinking of your card.'

I frowned, but did as he asked.

When I stopped spinning, I was a bit dizzy but Max was staring in total concentration. 'Is your card...' He paused to increase the drama. '...the TWO OF SPADES?!' He waved the two of spades at me.

'No,' I said.

'Really?' he asked.

'Positive.'

'In that case...' He plucked another card from the pack. 'It must be THE SIX OF HEARTS!'

I shook my head

'Ah – then it's...' He paused again. '...the NINE OF CLUBS!'

'Nope,' I said.

'Oh,' he said, disappointed, and shrugged. 'Funny – it always works with the cat.'

There was a long, awkward pause.

'Well, nice to meet you, Max.' I said eventually and walked back towards the cottage. He seemed like a nice enough kid – but not really the kind of person to go on adventures with.

'Wait!' he said.

I turned around.

'There *is* something else, actually...' He looked behind him, unsure. I stepped back towards him.

'Can you keep a secret?' he asked.

I hesitated. I always tried my absolute best to keep secrets, but sometimes they just slipped out. I nodded, though.

And then there was just birdsong, and the sound of leaves rustling in the gentle breeze. I wasn't sure if Max was going to continue. But then he said, in a voice not much louder than a whisper, 'Do you want to meet the tiny people that live at the bottom of my garden?'

CHAPTER THREE

I was speechless, which was very rare for me (ask Dad). I was guessing that Max had invented magical people to be his 'friends'. *I'd* often made up all sorts of creatures for my adventures too, so who was I to feel sorry for him? Plus, I had no friends here either. So, as he looked at me nervously, waiting for a reply, I played along.

'Okay, Max – take me to the "tiny people".'

He smiled, then raced to the end of his garden, towards the stream. I hurdled the low fence between our gardens and ran after him.

He stopped at the edge of the trickling water. It was pretty but was so narrow that you could cross it in one long stride, and only just deep enough to dip your toes in.

'I discovered the little people last summer when I caught one riding on Lola,' Max said, panting. Lola had followed us and was now weaving in and out of *my* legs, meowing. Her fur tickled my shins – it felt nice.

Tiny people that ride around on pets? Max's imagination seemed just as wild as mine. Maybe I'd misjudged him.

He stepped across the stream and stood proudly in front of a huge old tree. The trunk was so thick that even Dad couldn't have put his arms all the way around it, and so tall that the top branches – with dark green leaves – were higher than our roof.

'They live here,' he said, so I went up to

a low branch and gave the imaginary creatures a little wave.

'Well, hello there, tiny person. Max here tells me you are his "friend". How are you today?'

When I turned back, Max was staring at me like *I* was the weird one.

'Not *there*,' he said. '*Here*.' He pointed to the base of the tree, by the roots, and that's when I noticed the hole. It wasn't much bigger than a horseshoe, and was surrounded by beautiful, carved engravings of flowers. My eyes widened.

I knelt and looked closer – it was a doorway! And the door was wide open and beyond it was the strangest, most wonderful thing I had ever seen – a miniature room with tiny wooden furniture and walls covered in moss.

And then I gasped – because I saw them!

They'd been blending into the mossy walls: three little creatures, each no bigger than my thumb, and each with green skin, pointy ears and clear wings.

'The tiny people,' Max explained as he knelt next to me.

I looked at him and then back at the little creatures. My mouth was open so wide that one of the tiny people would have been able to fly in.

And then — just when I thought I couldn't possibly *be* any more shocked — one of the tiny creatures spoke. She had dark red hair tied up in a ponytail (the hair-tie was made from a single blade of grass).

'Oh, hello, Max,' she said, looking up at him and smiling. 'How nice of you to come see us again. But we've been through this — we're not "tiny people", we're *pixies.'*

'Sorry,' said Max, blushing. But then the pixies were all staring at *me*, and it was a long time before I was able to produce a single word.

'Pixies?' I squeaked.

Their wings began to flicker, their feet left the ground and they flew out of the room, one by one, towards me. As they all hovered in front of my face, they looked just as curious about *me* as I was about *them*.

The pixie who had spoken to Max said, 'A new human?'

'My friend,' said Max. 'Her name's Alice, she lives next door and she's eight.'

'And one month,' I added.

'It's so nice to meet you, Alice,' the pixie said. 'I'm Omfra.'

Her voice was soft and musical.

My heart was fluttering but eventually

a whole sentence managed to tumble out. 'I'm so thrilled to meet you, Omfra.'

'And I'm Bran,' announced another of the pixies, waving both hands at me. He was wearing a patchwork suit stitched together from leaves – greens and browns, reds and yellows. He looked me up and down. 'You don't look much like a human girl,' he said. 'And – is that a nest on your head?'

'Bran!' said Omfra. 'I'm so sorry, Alice. He always says the first thing that pops into his head, and it's often rude. I *love* your hair.'

But it was fine. I giggled.

'And this is Gillie,' said Omfra, nodding at the third pixie, who was hovering a bit further away than the other two. She had short orange hair and wore a tiny pair of glasses. 'Gillie loves humans too but she's rather shy.'

Gillie smiled at me but didn't speak.

'Hi, Gillie,' I said. 'Nice to meet you.'

She replied in the quietest, squeakiest voice I had ever heard. 'Hello, Alice.'

To all three of them, I gushed, 'I've read all about creatures like you! Like Tinkerbell and the Tooth Fairy – but I didn't think you were really real!'

Max blushed again and the pixies were now all frowning. 'Those creatures you mentioned,' explained Omfra, 'are *fairies*. NOT pixies.'

'**STUPID FAIRIES!**' yelled Bran. 'Boo to all fairies!'

'I'm sorry,' I said. 'I've always thought that pixies and fairies were kind of... the same thing.'

There was a really awkward silence. Bran was shaking his head. 'We're not even *slightly* the same. Are you the same as a chair? Is a berry the same as a hedgehog?'

'No,' I said. 'And no.'

'Correct,' he said. 'And pixies are *nothing* like fairies! We're kind and friendly and caring. Fairies are mean.'

Omfra nodded. 'Unlike fairies, pixies absolutely *love* humans. And we only use *our* magic for good.'

'We also love to travel and explore and learn things,' said Bran. 'The fairies? They don't think about anyone but themselves.'

Gillie flew closer to me. 'There are so many amazing creatures and trees and flowers all around us,' she said. 'And it's us pixies who look after them.'

Max grinned at me. 'Gillie's a real nature expert,' he said. 'You can ask her anything.'

Gillie blushed but looked up at me expectantly.

'Okay – what's *this* tree called?' I asked. 'The one you live in?'

'It's an oak,' she said proudly. 'It's such a wonderful tree, isn't it? Beautiful acorns grow on their branches and their trunks are so strong that you humans have used them to build huge houses and powerful ships.'

Maybe Max was right after all. Maybe trees *were* interesting.

'Pixies have lived in these woods for thousands of years,' said Omfra, 'but fairies have never liked us. And when you humans came along, the fairies didn't like *you* either! And now they want these woods all to themselves. Their queen, Tania, wants to force us all out – pixies *and* humans.'

'Boo to Queen Tania!' said Bran, and blew a raspberry.

Omfra said, 'I'm sorry about Bran's manners, Alice.'

'It's fine,' I said, smiling. 'I've got a baby brother who makes noises like that. And a dad too, actually.'

All three pixies laughed. So did Max.

I had so many things I wanted to ask the pixies: hundreds of questions all jumbled up in my head, fighting to get out.

Then: 'Alice!' It was my mum. She was standing just outside our back door, which was a long way away – but she had a Mum voice, so we could all hear her. 'Bath time!'

'What's a bath?' asked Bran.

'It's how humans wash,' said Omfra. 'They sit in a big tub of warm water, and...'

'Why don't they just jump in a stream?' he said. 'Or wait for it to rain?'

'Alice!' called Mum, a bit impatiently now. 'Come on, chicken!'

'Please, Mum – just five more minutes!'

'Nope!'

'*Three* more minutes?'

'Sorry!'

'Half a minute, then?!'

'Sure,' said Mum. 'I've started counting, though!'

But at least it gave me time to say goodbye to Max, and then I turned back to the pixies. 'Will you be here if we come back tomorrow?'

'Of course,' said Omfra, smiling. 'Where else would we be?'

CHAPTER FOUR

Even though it took me ages to get to sleep that night, my brain absolutely fizzing, I still managed to wake up early the next morning. I got dressed in no time and rushed into the kitchen to sneak out through the back door. I'd thought everyone was still asleep – the house was quiet – but Dad was in his dressing gown, sitting at the kitchen table with a book and a cup of tea.

'Morning,' he said, surprised to see me. 'You're up early. Breakfast?'

I shook my head. 'No time.' And I kept on going towards the back door.

But Dad shook *his* head, smiling. 'There's always time for breakfast, Alice. Even adventurers need breakfast. *Especially* adventurers.'

So I grabbed a banana from the fruit bowl, peeled it and gobbled it up in about ten seconds.

Dad watched on, astonished, then grinned. 'Why are you in such a hurry? I thought there was nothing to do around here.'

'Adventures,' I said.

'Great,' he said. I plopped the banana peel in the bin and waved goodbye.

Max was already down the bottom of the garden, waiting for me. But when I got closer, I saw that he was frowning.

'They're gone!' he said.

'The pixies?'

He nodded.

We hopped across the stream, raced up to the big oak and crouched in front of it. Sure enough, the door was wide open but nobody was home.

'Bran! Omfra! Gillie!' I called. When there was no reply, I turned to Max. 'Maybe they've just gone out to...' And that's when I realised I had absolutely no idea what pixies did all day.

'They're *always* here when I come to visit,' Max said. 'And I've looked all over. Plus, they wouldn't have left the door wide open, would they – if they were all out? Something must have happened.'

'Maybe we can track their footprints,' I suggested, peering at the ground.

Max shook his head. 'They usually prefer to fly.'

'Right,' I said, feeling a bit silly. 'Of course they do. So?'

He shrugged and said, 'We'll just have to wait.'

I wasn't happy about this, but he was probably right. We both sat by the stream, too disappointed to speak. Max took out his pack of cards and shuffled them distractedly. I dipped a hand into the cold water and, after a while, with nothing else to do,

I asked him questions. All of them were pixie-related, of course. And all his answers were disappointingly short.

Yes, there were lots of other pixies in the fields around here – but no, he'd never actually met any of them. He'd never seen a fairy, either – but this wasn't really a surprise because, according to Omfra, fairies stayed away from humans as much as possible.

I was super-jealous of all the time that Max had spent with the pixies – but I hoped I didn't let it show. When I ran out of questions, I told him about where I used to live and about my old friends there, and about Oscar. But compared to the pixies, none of it felt very interesting any more.

Then there was the softest of noises – the fluttering of tiny wings. I looked up.

The pixies! All three of them were flying towards us: Omfra in front, Bran next, zig-zagging, and Gillie, trying to keep up.

'You're back!' I yelped.

Max and I leapt to our feet.

But when they were close enough that we could see their expressions, it was clear that something was badly wrong.

'What's happened?' I asked.

'It's the fairies!' said Omfra. 'They've frozen our queen! They used a powerful spell, and nothing that we tried could unfreeze her.'

'Even tickling didn't work,' Bran added sadly.

'A pixie queen?' I said.

'Her Majesty Queen Joan of all the Pixies!' said Bran breathlessly. 'She's super-nice — even by pixie standards.'

'And they *froze* her?' I said. 'Why?'

'Because the fairies want the fields to themselves,' said Omfra. 'They must think that, without our queen to protect us, we'll be too afraid to stay.'

'Which is probably true,' said Gillie sadly.

'And when they've driven us pixies out,' Omfra continued, 'they'll drive out all the creatures, and then the humans.'

'They're always up to something,' said Bran, shaking his head.

'But they've never gone this far before,' added Omfra. Yesterday, she'd seemed super-calm — like nothing could bother her. Right now, though, she was really upset.

'Can we bargain with them?' I suggested. 'Whenever Dad wants me to clean my room, he promises me something nice after — like a hot chocolate with marshmallows floating on top, getting all gooey.'

'Yum,' said Max.

'You could promise the fairies hot chocolate if they unfreeze Queen Joan,' I said.

But Omfra shook her head sadly.

'Don't fairies like hot chocolate?' I said.

'Of course they do!' said Bran. 'Everyone likes hot chocolate.'

'But fairies just can't be bargained with,'

said Omfra. 'However much we try.'

Now Max had an idea. 'Could we unfreeze her using something warm? My grandma has a hot-water bottle.'

'If only, Max,' said Omfra kindly. 'Queen Joan is not frozen in a *cold* way, however, like an ice cream. She's frozen like a statue. And I'm afraid that only magic can bring her back.'

'But *you* can do magic, right?' I said to Omfra. 'Can't you undo the spell?'

'Pixie magic is much weaker than

fairy magic,' she said with a sigh. 'For example, while we need these wings of ours to fly, fairies can fly without wings. And fairy spells – the strongest ones – are hidden in a heavily guarded room in their tree-palace.'

'Can you go there, then?' I asked. 'To find the spell?'

'Great idea!' said Bran. He turned to Omfra. 'We can dress up like fairies – me, you and Gillie – sneak into the palace, find the spell room, get past the guards, and...'

Omfra shook her head. 'We're *green*,' she said. 'And we've got wings. Just one look at us, and they'll know we're pixies – and then we'll get frozen too.'

Bran's shoulders slumped. But Gillie whispered into Omfra's ear.

'That's a great idea!' said Omfra. Gillie glowed with pride. '*We* can't get into the fairy tree-palace because we are – quite clearly – pixies. But... *you two* could!'

She was looking at me and Max.

'But we're *enormous*,' I said. 'We'd never fit into a fairy house. Not even a fairy *palace*.'

Omfra nodded. 'That's perfectly true, Alice. But, while pixie magic might not be fairy-strength,' she said, 'we can do *some* magical things.'

'Like what?' I said.

'Like – we can shrink things. We could turn you both fairy-size!'

Chapter Five

As we followed the pixies to their oak tree, my heart was racing: at last, a real-life adventure!

But Max didn't seem so enthusiastic. 'Won't it hurt?' he said. 'Being shrunk?'

'Not even a bit,' said Bran, but Max still wasn't convinced:

'How do *you* know?'

'Because,' said Bran proudly, 'I once shrunk myself to the size of a pea.'

'Why?' I asked.

Bran shrugged. 'I was bored. Don't you sometimes get bored?'

'Yes — but I don't shrink myself pea-sized. I just make up adventures. Or read a book.'

Bran turned to Max. 'Anyway, it felt really nice,' he said. 'Being shrunk.'

But Max still looked worried. 'I think I'll stay here,' he mumbled, 'and guard the pixie house.'

'Come on, Max,' I said brightly. 'These pixies need our help.'

Max shook his head. 'Too dangerous.'

Omfra nodded — she'd obviously changed her mind. 'You're quite right, Max. It's far too dangerous. If the fairies realise that you're humans, they'll freeze *you* too — or worse.'

I didn't want to imagine what was worse than being frozen, but I said, 'We *love* danger. Don't we, Max?'

'Not really,' he said.

'And if we don't help,' I added eagerly to Omfra, 'your queen will stay frozen, right?'

Omfra nodded sadly.

'And you pixies will probably have to leave the fields, and then the fairies will start work on getting us humans out...'

She nodded again.

'Right,' I said, turning to Max. 'I can do this by myself – if you don't want to come. But adventures are much more fun with a friend.'

Max sighed deeply and – eventually – nodded.

'Are you both absolutely sure?' asked Omfra.

I nodded enthusiastically.

Max nodded not quite so enthusiastically.

'Wonderful!' she said. 'Ready?'

'Yes,' I said, and she pulled a tiny wooden wand, no bigger than a splinter, from her belt and pointed it at us.

The first thing I knew, my skin

was tingling all over — this warm, tickly feeling. Then my hands and feet were trembling, my fingers and toes wiggling and my breathing fast. Then everything was a blur: I spun and spun — a dizzy feeling — and my feet left the ground. I landed with a bump on my bottom in the grass in front of their house.

Max landed next to me, moments later. He was also dizzy — and tiny. 'Wow!' he said.

And 'Wow!' was all *I* could say, too.

The pixies helped us to our feet and led us inside their house.

It was strange seeing them up close like this. I noticed new things: Omfra had streaks of silver in her dark red hair, Gillie had freckles and Bran had a thin scar on his cheek, which he was scratching as he stared at Max and me.

'Well,' he said, 'you're the right size for fairies — and you definitely aren't green. But fairies are *never* scruffy.'

'Hey,' I said crossly. 'I washed my hair last night.'

'It must have been a very quick wash,' Bran said (which was true).

Max chuckled, but stopped when Bran said, 'And *your* hair's even messier.'

Then Bran bustled over to a big chest in

the corner (which had seemed so tiny before), flung it open, rummaged around, pulled out a tiny pine cone and strode over to us.

'A pine-comb,' he said. 'To get those tangles out.'

I flinched. I never let Dad near my hair because he's too rough with any knots. To my surprise, though, Bran was actually gentle — more like Mum. Then he worked on Max's red hair, which was wiry and so took a bit longer.

'That's the hair taken care of,' said Bran. 'Now, for the clothes.'

He went back over to the chest and, hunched over, threw an assortment of colourful material behind him in search of something.

'Aha!' he exclaimed.

Bran held out what looked like two shimmery purple pieces of cloth — which, on closer inspection, were petals. In a flurry of movement, he worked on them with a pair of wooden scissors, a pine needle and some silk thread. After a whirl of snipping and stitching, he stood back to admire his work.

'Dresses?' said Max.

'*Robes*, actually,' said Bran. 'All fairies wear them. Try them on.'

We did — they fit perfectly. (And being made from petals, they were wonderfully soft and smelt nice too.)

I did a twirl. So did Max.

'You both look great!' said Omfra. We giggled.

But Bran wasn't so sure. '*Fairy* robes,' he said, 'are made with the finest material — not petals. But as long as they don't look too closely, you should be okay.'

Gillie whispered in his ear.

'Oh yes,' he said. 'The finishing touch.'

He rushed back to the chest and returned with two strange-looking headbands made of painted wood.

'You'll need these,' he announced. 'Tiaras.'

'Aren't they supposed to be sparkly?' I said.

'Yes,' Bran admitted. 'But it's the best I could do. The fairies keep all the sparkly things to themselves.'

(I decided that, when I got home, I'd go to my craft box and find some glitter to bring him.)

Max put his tiara on, and so did I.

'They're great,' I said, trying to make Bran feel better.

Omfra smiled and said, 'It's time to go.'

CHAPTER SIX

Was I ready? Everything was moving so fast. And Max looked even more nervous than me. 'How would we even get there, anyway?' he asked.

'At the top of this tree,' said Omfra calmly, 'is a long twisty vine—'

'Which works like a slide!' interrupted Bran excitedly. 'We call it The Whoosh and it's the absolute best thing ever. It goes round and round and this way and that way and up and down, super-fast and...'

'Sounds scary,' Max muttered.

'It's fun!' said Bran. 'It lands in fairy territory

and the best thing is, they don't even know it's there, so we can sneak in.'

'But we almost *never* go near the palace,' said Omfra, 'and we only ever visit fairy territory in absolute emergencies.'

Bran had a guilty look, which made me think that he sometimes used The Whoosh in *non*-emergencies.

'But — how will we get to the top of the tree?' asked Max.

I'd been wondering that too. Because climbing to the top of this huge oak would be difficult and dangerous if we were normal-size — even for an experienced cardboard-box-climber like me. Getting to the top of this tree now that we were *small* would be pretty much impossible.

'The thing is,' said Max, 'I think I might be afraid of heigh...'

Before he could finish his sentence, Gillie clutched his hand, Bran grabbed my hand and we were jolted off our feet and zooming out of the pixie house, up into the sky.

I gasped and then — when I'd caught my breath — let out an enormous squeal of joy. '**WHEEEEEE!**'

Max, meanwhile, was screaming in terror: '**AAAAARRRGGGHHH!**'

We followed Omfra as she flew up and up, swerving in and out of branches, dodging leaves. Our robes rippled and the breeze rushed over our faces. We were flying! It was incredible! (Though the higher I got, the tighter I gripped Bran's hand.) I was yelling '**YiPPEEEEEE!**', and only stopped when we landed on a branch at the top. It was wide enough that I didn't worry about tumbling off.

Max and Gillie landed next to us. Max wasn't nearly so calm.

'You seem a bit nervous,' I said.

'A bit?' he said. 'A bit?! I'm *terrified*! We're balanced on a branch that's higher than my roof! We're so tiny that a bird might mistake us for breakfast...'

'Ah – don't worry about that,' said Gillie softly. 'Pixies and birds are friends. We help them sometimes, and *they* help *us*.'

At that moment, I was feeling a bit like a bird myself – the view from up here was spectacular. I gazed down at the treetops and the fields and hedges far below. I saw the roofs of our house and Max's house and, in the distance, I could just make out a thin band of blue – the sea!

It was all just *magical*.

But Max shuffled nearer the edge of the

branch and inspected the vine.

'The Whoosh!' said Bran proudly. It *did* look like a slide, kind of, but one of those twisty, turny, terrifying slides at a waterpark — the kind of ride you have to be a really big kid or a grown-up to go on. And with those slides, even the scariest ones, they were always safe. But The Whoosh weaved in and out of branches and seemed to disappear.

Omfra noticed my expression. 'You're nervous, Alice?'

'A bit,' I said.

'A *bit*?!' said Max again. 'You want us to go down *there*? And if we somehow survive *that* — we have to sneak into the fairy tree-palace and find the spell! And if we get found out, we'll get frozen ourselves! Or worse!'

There was a long silence. The only sound

was the breeze rustling leaves all around us. I looked down at the hundreds of trees and said, 'How will we know where the tree-palace is?'

'It's in a Norway spruce,' said Gillie. 'You humans would call it a Christmas tree: it's so

tall and glamorous, like the fairies themselves. And the palace inside is *huge*.'

Bran blew a raspberry.

Omfra sighed at him, then looked at me and Max. 'Are you completely sure about this?' she said.

I nodded. Max did too, but much less confidently. I was worried he would change his mind or try to talk me out of going – so, without saying another word and without even waving goodbye, I jumped on to The Whoosh.

I whooshed.

CHAPTER SEVEN

I hurtled down The Whoosh, twisting one way and the other, looping and swerving, dipping and curving. It was like the most incredible rollercoaster. I was sliding so fast that it felt like my tummy and my heart were swapping places. I squealed pretty much the whole way down – part 'squeal of joy', part 'squeal of terror' – until I crashed on to my bottom into a soft patch of moss, like a crash-mat at gymnastics.

I took a while to catch my breath and I'd only just got to my feet when I heard a loud '**AAAAAAARRRRGGGGHHHH!**' and saw Max whooshing down and hitting the moss beside me. He lay there on his back for ages, panting and staring up at me. Then he said, 'That was **AWESOME!**'

He was completely right — it was the most exciting thing I'd ever done in my entire life. Even now, a minute after landing, my heart was still thumping.

'What next?' said Max eventually.

'We look for the fairy-tree palace,' I said, and sniffed. 'I can smell Christmas trees — so we might be close. Now, the important thing is to blend in. We're fairies, remember.'

'Right,' said Max. He frowned. 'How do fairies walk, again?'

I tried to picture how fairies moved in films and did my best impression of an elegant walk – on tiptoes, my head tilted back, my chin in the air. Max copied me.

We waded through the grass (which would have been really short if we'd been normal-sized but now it came up to our tummies). We clambered over pebbles, which seemed to us like boulders, and avoided an earthworm, which seemed like a massive pink snake. Max squeaked in terror. The worm wriggled away.

And then we squirmed our way through a bush that was blocking our path and – on the other side – we saw an open door in the base of a tree. This wasn't a Christmas tree – and it definitely wasn't the palace. The door was small and unguarded. But inside were three fairies, all in sparkly robes, and all jostling for position in front of a big mirror on the far wall.

'It's *my* turn, Morgan!' said the first fairy to the second one.

'But you've been hogging the mirror for *ages*, Finn!' snapped Morgan.

And the third fairy – a bit smaller than the first two – just sighed and gave up.

Finn – with short, dark hair, brown eyes and dressed in silver – must have glimpsed us in the reflection, because he spun around and, frowning, said, 'Ex*cuse* me, who are YOU?'

'I'm Alice,' I said, a lot more confidently than I was feeling. And because Max was too nervous to say anything, I added, 'And this is Max.'

Max stared at the fairies like he was a startled rabbit, but then raised a hand and gave them a  little wave.

Morgan, whose gold outfit was the sparkliest of all and whose perfectly straight blonde hair went right down to her bottom, was glaring at us. 'And — *what* are you?' she said. 'Because you're certainly not fairies.'

'We *are*,' I said indignantly.

'Well, you don't *look* much like fairies,' said Finn. 'And I've never seen you before.'

I had to think fast. 'We're from another field,' I said. 'We're just visiting.'

'There can't be many sparkles in your field,' said Morgan dismissively, looking at our robes.

'There aren't,' I said.

'Or brushes or combs, by the look of it,' she added rudely.

That's when I noticed our reflections in the big mirror. The Whoosh had blown our hair around *a lot*. (And struggling through the bush probably hadn't helped either.) I blushed.

Finn stepped over for a closer look, and turned to Morgan. 'They're not so much fairies,' he said, 'as '*fairlies*'. They're only *fairly* well-dressed. *Fairly* well-groomed. *Fairly* attractive.'

Morgan laughed. I groaned.

My friends back at my old school absolutely **WORSHIPPED** fairies. They dressed up as them for fancy-dress parties and covered their schoolbooks in fairy stickers. They believed that fairies were beautiful and kind and would always be helpful to humans.

And, yes, these fairies *were* beautiful. But the pixies had been right: they were also selfish and vain, and they seemed really mean.

All three of them were eyeing us suspiciously and I tried to think how I could convince them that we were real fairies. What did fairies like? Or rather, what did fairies *not* like...? I had an idea.

'How about those pixies, eh?' I said, putting my hand on my hip and trying to look cool and unimpressed. 'We just met some and they were so... smelly.' Max turned to me, horrified, until he realised what I was doing.

'Yeah,' he added, sticking his hand on his hip too. 'And they are so... short! And green!'

'That is so true,' said Finn. 'Smelly and short and soooo plain.'

'Don't forget dull,' said Morgan. 'All they care about are plants and creepy-crawlies and animals.'

'And those horrible giant humans,' Finn added.

The third fairy – in a sparkly blue outfit – finally spoke. 'Yeah,' she said. 'Pixies, hey? They're pretty bad. Except, I met one once who was actually quite nice.'

The other two glared at her.

'Shush, Dana,' said Morgan.

Dana shrank into herself a little.

But at least the fairies seemed to have accepted us.

'You're just in time, strange fairies,' Finn announced. 'Queen Tania is throwing a ball today to celebrate our great victory over those pesky pixies.'

'Victory?' I said.

'She FROZE Queen Joan!' explained Morgan. 'Ha! Now their "leader" can't lead them – she just sits on her sad little throne all day looking silly.' She laughed. Finn joined in.

Dana said, 'Would you two like to come to the ball with us?'

Thinking that this would be a great way to get into the palace, I said, 'Yes, please!'

Morgan scrunched up her face as if she'd just eaten something sour. 'Well, you'll have to stand right at the back, looking like *that*.

Queen Tania only likes *beautiful* things.'

Looking embarrassed by the other fairies' rudeness, Dana said, 'Would you both like a cupcake?' She stepped over to the table, picked up a china plate and offered us two of the most perfectly iced pink-and-yellow cupcakes I had ever seen.

'Oh yes please,' said Max.

'Thank you so much,' I said.

'It's my own recipe-spell,' she said shyly. 'Would you like one, Morgan?'

'Yuck, no, Dana. *Stop* offering me those disgusting creations of yours,' Morgan replied. Dana blushed.

Maybe the pixies weren't *completely* right about fairies, after all, because Dana actually seemed quite nice.

I took a bite from my cupcake. It was absolutely delicious! Like strawberries and ice cream somehow turned into a cake, with toffee-flavoured popping candy on the top. I don't think even Dad could have made something so tasty.

'I think your cake is wonderful, Dana,' I said to her. She blushed.

Beside me, Max had finished his already and his face was covered in yellow crumbs and pink icing. 'Umm... hmm... nom-nom,' he said, with a mouthful of cake. He gave Dana a double thumbs-up.

Finn and Morgan, meanwhile, were staring into the mirror, making sure that every single hair was in place.

'How do I look?' said Morgan, swishing her long blonde hair dramatically.

'Fine,' said Finn.

'I don't want to look "fine",' Morgan huffed. '"Fine" might be okay for Dana – but not for *me*.'

Dana sighed. 'I can hear you both, you know.'

'With *those* ears,' said Finn, 'I'm not surprised.'

Dana's shoulders slumped. I was about to say how nice she looked, but a trumpet sounded in the distance. Max jumped. The fairies looked at each other excitedly.

'It's starting!' squealed Finn. 'The ball!'

And then they were off – out of the door and floating just above the ground, with surprising speed and grace. Max and I followed them on tiptoes, doing our best fairy-walk and trying to keep up.

CHAPTER EIGHT

The pixies had been right about the fairies' tree-palace: it was in the biggest, most incredible Christmas tree I'd ever seen and, looking through the entrance as we approached, two guards wearing pearly armour. My heart was racing again — would these guards believe we were real fairies?

'Who are *they*?' one of the guards asked the fairies, nodding at me and Max.

'They're our friends from a different field,' said Dana.

'I wouldn't expect *you* to know them,'

said Finn to the guard, 'because you have no friends.'

The guard looked sulky but stood aside and let us through — into a huge, fancy hall. The ceiling was high and curved, and it was the shiniest room I had ever been in, so shiny that it made Max and I squint. The floor was made from pearls and the walls were covered in pieces of silver that looked suspiciously like human jewellery.

And then there were the fairies — at least a hundred of them, floating around just off the ground or standing in small groups, chatting. *They* sparkled too, elegant and beautiful — and you could tell from their expressions that they completely knew it.

'Wow!' said Max. 'So many fairies!'

'Shh!' I whispered. 'You'll give us away.'

'Sorry.'

Along the walls were brightly coloured doors leading to rooms with curious signs.

'Unicorns?!' I said, unable to hide my excitement. 'They *exist*?!'

'Shh,' said Max. 'You'll give us away.'

I blushed and nodded. I'd deserved that.

I was trying to work out where the spell-room might be — and Finn must have seen me glancing around, because he said, 'Impressive, isn't it? The palace. I bet there's nothing like it in *your* non-sparkly field.'

This gave me an idea.

'In the tree-palace in *my* field,' I said, 'there's an entire room full of spells. I bet you don't have one of those.'

'We most certainly do,' he said huffily, and pointed towards it. 'It's hidden away, next to the unicorn grooming parlour.'

Before I could tell Max what I'd discovered,

I was jolted by what sounded like a thousand flutes playing at once. All of the fairies fell silent and turned to face a high, circular stage in the centre of the hall.

An incredibly tall fairy, with perfect golden curls, a dazzling tiara and a shimmery purple robe floated on to the stage. The other fairies let out a collective 'oooh' and bowed gracefully towards her.

'She's so shiny,' Max whispered. 'She hurts my eyes.'

'**ALL HAIL QUEEN TANIA!**' announced an important-looking fairy. '**THE FAIREST AND SPARKLIEST AND WISEST QUEEN IN THE WORLD.**'

There was a huge round of applause from the fairies. Max and I joined in so that we didn't stand out.

'My fairies!' cried Tania. 'We are gathered

here today to drink sparkly juice and eat
fancy cakes in celebration of our brilliant
victory over those infuriating little pixies!'

There was a massive cheer, and applause,
but the queen was looking cross.

'I haven't finished yet!' she yelled, and
the fairies immediately fell silent. 'Now that

their awful queen is a statue, those ugly pixies will finally leave! And never again will we have to look at those silly green pests!'

There was another enormous cheer from the fairies. Finn was hopping up and down, looking like he might explode with excitement.

'**I STILL HAVEN'T FINISHED!**' yelled Tania, stamping her silver heel on the pearly stage. The fairies were quiet again.

'And with the pixies gone,' she continued, 'we can finally get rid of those awful **HUMANS** – who are forever trampling everything and getting in the way and, what is more, have **NO SENSE OF STYLE!**'

There was an awkward silence, with the fairies not sure if she'd finished, until Queen Tania announced, 'You are now free to applaud!'

They did – and cheered and whooped.

I looked at Max, rolled my eyes, and then nodded. We slipped away from the crowd – to find the spell-room.

CHAPTER NINE

I led the way, passing tall, colourful doors on either side.

'Look!' said Max, pointing further along. A door opened, there was a bright glowing light, and something was trotting towards us.

At first, I thought it was a tiny, white horse. And then I saw the horn on its head.

'A unicorn!' I gasped. 'They're really real!'

Even after all that we'd seen and done so far on this adventure — meeting the pixies, being shrunk, The Whoosh, the fairies and now this incredible palace — the sight of an actual *unicorn* completely took my breath away. Its coat was a dazzling snow-white, its mane a glittering pink and its silver horn seemed to glow.

'So, that room must be the unicorn vet that Finn told me about,' I whispered as the unicorn trotted past us. 'He said it's right next to the spell-room.'

'Come on, then,' Max said, and we both broke into a run.

Two doors down from the unicorn parlour was a glitter-powder room and between those rooms was a very narrow, sparkly turquoise door, with a star sign above it.

I really wanted to look inside *all* the rooms. But we had a job to do – and a pixie queen to save. 'A star is a symbol for magic, right?' I said. 'So the spell book must be in here!'

But then, as were about to enter, I heard a shout from behind us.

'Oi, badly dressed new fairies!'

We turned to see Finn, Morgan and Dana staring at us.

'What are you two up to?' said Finn suspiciously.

My mind went completely blank. But Max came to the rescue. 'We were looking for *you*!' he said.

'Huh?' said Finn.

'I've got something to show you. Something magic. Come this way.'

Max winked at me, then turned and marched off down the corridor, with the three fairies following him.

I turned back towards the tall, turquoise door. Max had provided the distraction. Now I had to do *my* bit and find that spell.

Checking that no one was watching me, I pushed open the door and slipped into the spell-room. It was surprisingly big, brightly lit and cluttered with fancy furniture. But my eyes were drawn to a huge glittering book displayed on a dark wooden stand high up in the centre of the room. Clearly it was only meant to be touched by creatures who could fly.

I scanned the room, looking more closely at the silver tables and velvet chairs, the wooden wardrobes and plump armchairs.

Dad had stopped me from reaching the

top of Mount Cardboard yesterday, but there was no one here to stop me climbing – not yet, at least.

I clambered on to a chair, and from there stepped on to a high table – then leapt on to the top of a wardrobe. It creaked. I wobbled – and glimpsed the hard stone floor below – but didn't fall.

My legs were shaking. Real-life adventures were a lot scarier than make-believe ones, that was for sure. But I took a deep breath and reminded myself that I was a born adventurer – *I could do this*. From the wardrobe, I jumped over to the tower. I squealed, but clung on and – straining every muscle – pulled my way to the top!

There was no flag to plant at the top of *this* climb, but there was something much more important: I had a spell to find.

The book was much bigger up close, bright gold and covered in gemstones and diamonds – the most incredible object I'd ever seen. I ran my fingers over the silver letters that spelt out the name of the book:

COMPLETE SPELLS, POTIONS AND ASSORTED MAGIC... FOR FAIRY EYES ONLY!

It was mesmerising. For a second, I forgot why I was here. Then I focused.

I heaved the book open and studied the contents page.

That's when I heard a commotion outside the door – muffled voices and rustling robes. I guessed I didn't have much time, so I flicked furiously through the pages to get to the unfreezing spell.

And there it was. I didn't have a pen or pencil to write it down so, as much as I hated to damage such a beautiful book, I knew I'd have to tear out the page. But, when I tried to rip it out, nothing happened. The paper was untearable. The book itself was obviously magic.

I groaned. What could I do? The book was much too heavy to carry. So I'd have to try to *memorise* the spell.

I read it over and over, trying to suck the words from the page into my head. Then I remembered something that my teacher, Mrs Lim, had taught me, and concentrated super-hard.

But the door burst open. I flinched — and lost balance, plummeting towards the hard floor. Luckily I landed on an armchair, but the fall still knocked the wind out of me. As I was struggling for breath, Max and the three fairies were staring down at me. Max looked sheepish.

'So,' said Finn coldly. 'You're both **HUMANS!**'

CHAPTER TEN

'Humans,' said Morgan, shaking her head and pulling a face.

'Humans who've been *shrunk*,' said Finn. 'No doubt by pixies!'

Max's guilty look gave this away.

'I should have known you weren't fairies,' said Morgan, glaring at me. 'You have such awful hair. And your friend there tried to distract us with his "magic trick", which is when we realised that he wasn't magic **AT ALL**. It was just an ordinary pack of playing cards. And he didn't even guess the right card!'

'It usually works with the cat,' mumbled Max.

'And,' Morgan continued, 'a *real* fairy wouldn't need to climb to reach the spell book.' She pulled out a silver wand and waggled it in our direction. To Max she said, 'Behold some *real* magic, human. A handy little spell I know

— to turn people into apples.'

Max gulped. 'I like apples,' he admitted. 'But I don't want to *be* one.'

Morgan ignored him and began to recite the spell. 'Prepare for joy! Prepare for laughter! Make these humans apple-y ever after!'

As Morgan was about to zap us with her wand, I squeezed Max's hand and prepared for my new life as an apple.

'Wait!'

It was Dana.

'What is it?' snapped Morgan.

'Shouldn't we take them to Queen Tania so *she* can decide what to do with them?' said Dana. 'She might not want them to be apples. And she might be angry if you make a decision without her.'

Morgan, for the first time, hesitated. She looked angry with us and annoyed with Dana, but she also seemed scared of getting in trouble with her queen. She sighed, and put her wand away – for now, at least.

Max and I looked at each other, incredibly relieved not to be fruit. But we were still trapped. And, as I'd just discovered, Queen Tania had a whole book full of mean spells she could use to punish us. Would we be turned into something really horrible – like nettles, or broccoli? Or would we have to suffer eternal tickles?

Max was terrified. I held his hand, feeling guilty that I'd talked him into joining me on what looked to be our first and last real adventure. I was really scared too.

Maybe I wouldn't get to see my parents or my baby brother ever again.

I was trying to come up with a plan, but there was no way that we'd get past these three fairies – and even if we did, there were a hundred more fairies in the palace who could capture us, and then there were the guards at the door.

'Any ideas?' I whispered.

Max – surprisingly – nodded and, in his loudest voice, yelled, 'LOLA!'

The fairies stared at him. I'll admit it – so did I.

'I've been trying to train Lola,' he whispered to me, 'for a magic trick I've been working on.'

'Lola the cat?' I whispered back.

He nodded.

'But cats,' I pointed out, 'just like little brothers, are almost impossible to train.'

'My grandma says that "impossible" spells "I'm possible". And cats have really good hearing.'

'So, when you call Lola, does she usually come?'

He shook his head.

'Ever?' I asked.

'No,' he whispered. 'Not so far, anyway.'

I sighed.

Morgan grabbed me roughly by the arm, Finn took hold of Max, and Dana looked on apologetically as they marched us out of the spell room and along the corridor, towards the great hall. It was a long way and by the time we reached Queen Tania, all the fairies in the palace knew about us and what we'd been up to.

A sparkly but very angry crowd had gathered around us.

I realised there would be absolutely no chance of escape.

Queen Tania was hovering just above us, her face crimson with rage.

'Humans!' she boomed. 'Your crimes are as follows: imitating fairies!' (The crowd of fairies booed.) 'Attempting to steal spells!' (More boos.) 'Spying on behalf of pixies!' (Very loud boos.) 'Messy hair!'

(More boos, but this last one felt a bit harsh.)

'Your punishment,' she said. 'You shall both be turned into beetles!'

Max yelped. 'I'm scared of beetles!'

I frowned at him. 'But you'll *be* a beetle.'

He yelped again. 'Then I'll be scared of myself!'

I held his hand, preparing for the worst. Queen Tania pointed her sparkly wand at us. And...

That's when we heard a deafening '**MIIIAAAOOOW!**', followed closely by lots of screams and squeals — and the fairies were no longer surrounding us, but flitting around, terrified, trying to hide.

I spun around and saw — here in the hall, blocking the entrance — Lola.

And, on Lola's back, clinging on with one hand and waving at us with the other: Bran.

CHAPTER ELEVEN

In all the pandemonium, Bran hopped off Lola, swooped down and landed next to us.

I was so stunned that I could only splutter single words, not actual sentences. 'How? What? Why?'

Bran was in such a hurry that all his words bumped into each other. 'We saw Lola hurtling over from your garden, Max, so we guessed you were in trouble. I jumped on board for the ride. Now – quick – take my hands and we'll get up on Lola and get her to take us out of...'

But a panicking fairy crashed into Bran

and sent him sprawling. And then something even worse happened: Queen Tania was right in front of us.

'A spell!' she yelled. 'To make a sound! I summon' – she jabbed her wand furiously in Lola's direction – 'the bark of a hound!'

Out of nowhere came a huge, rumbling **'WOOOOOOOOFFFFFFFFF!'**

Lola let out a screech of panic, spun around and bolted out of the palace, knocking over several fairies as she did and racing away through the forest.

Now that Lola had gone, the fairies had stopped squealing and Queen Tania was much calmer too.

She smoothed her robe, patted down her curly golden hair and advanced menacingly towards us, smiling horribly. 'A pixie is behind this,' she said. 'I knew it.' To me, she added, 'Looking for the unfreezing spell, by any chance?'

I couldn't help myself. 'Yes,' I said. 'And I found it too.'

'You did?' said Bran, excitedly.

But Queen Tania laughed. 'It makes no difference,' she said, 'whether you found it or not. Beetles can't use spells, can they? They can only do beetle-y things, like scuttling around – and being squashed underfoot.'

She demonstrated – with a heel of her sparkly shoes – just how she would do that.

Max yelped.

'And now for the spell – no longer for *two*

beetles, but for three.' She sneered at Bran, who gulped, and she pointed her wand at us, one at a time. 'Eeny-meeny-miny-mo, into beetles you shall... **OUCH!**'

Her crooked smile turned into a grimace of pain. She spun around, rubbing her bottom.

We could see that Omfra and Gillie were behind her, their wooden wands held out.

'You poked me in the **BOTTOM!**' Queen Tania screamed. 'How dare you! Do you *know* what we do to pixies who dare enter this palace?'

Omfra and Gillie weren't waiting around to find out – they were already flying away, heading for the exit.

'Quick,' said Bran, darting over to us. We clasped a hand each and he swept us off the ground and the three of us were flying after the other pixies

Queen Tania was still stunned for a moment and rubbing her bottom, but soon found her voice. 'Fairies!' she yelled. 'Don't let them escape! Capture them!'

Gillie and Omfra – in front of us – darted and swerved to avoid being caught by angry fairies. The two guards at the entrance both made a grab for them, but crashed into each other. So it looked like we were going to escape too – but Finn, Morgan and Dana were blocking the exit.

'Bad luck, fairlies,' said Morgan, reaching

out to grab us. Finn reached out too.

But Dana had one foot on each of their robes and, pinned to the ground, Morgan and Finn couldn't quite get us.

'Dana, you clumsy goat!' yelled Morgan.

'Move!' snapped Finn.

'Oh – sorry!' said Dana. 'I must have got my foot tangled.'

As we flew past, she caught my eye and gave me a small smile.

We hurtled out of the fairy tree-palace and soared away. 'Phew!' I said. 'That was close!'

But when I glanced over my shoulder, I saw that a fairy was chasing us. Queen Tania herself. And, even worse, she was *fast*. Much faster than us.

'She's right behind us!' I yelled. Everyone looked around, and even Omfra looked terrified.

But a huge shadow fell over all of us. I gasped, and looked up to see a bird with long brown wings and a grey belly flying above us, the white tip of its tail glinting in the sun.

'Queen Tania might be faster than a pixie,' said Gillie. 'But she's *not* faster than a turtle dove.'

Just behind us I heard Tania let out a frightened scream. 'What is that monstrous beast?' she cried.

'This is Adar,' said Gillie. 'She's a turtle dove. We helped her once – she hurt a wing – and now she's helping us.'

Adar swooped underneath us so that we could land safely on her back, and flapped a wing in Tania's direction to create a powerful gust of wind. The fairy queen was blown straight back towards her palace, her robes and perfect hair flying about in a mess. Her frustrated squeal was lost in the wind.

Chapter Twelve

Now that Queen Tania was no longer coming for us, I could properly enjoy the flight. I grasped Adar's feathers to hold on tight, but she didn't seem to mind — she was soaring high above the treetops, gliding in a slow arc. The wind was whipping through our hair and was cool on our faces as the trees and flowers whooshed by beneath us. I glanced at Max. He was holding on just as tightly but he seemed to be having fun too, grinning widely and letting out a loud '**WOOO-HOOOO!**'

I gazed at the forest below us, and Gillie

must have noticed the look of wonder on my face.

'They're beautiful, aren't they?' she said. 'The trees?'

I nodded.

'Those are elms,' she said, pointing. 'Some of them are hundreds of years old. And those beautiful pinkish flowers down there – rhododendrons. And there, in the heather, is where rabbits live. And... hang on tight!'

I squealed, my tummy lurching – Adar swooped down and landed with a bump on a patch of clear ground. We all jumped off and thanked her for saving us. Adar cooed, and took off powerfully. Soon she was out of sight and we were all standing outside a majestic tree with a twisty trunk and covered with dark green leaves and red berries.

'Isn't it amazing?' said Gillie. 'It's a yew tree — one of the oldest in England. The perfect home for a pixie queen, don't you think?'

We walked inside through the carved entrance. Queen Joan's castle was much smaller and cosier than the fairies' grand palace, and decorated with acorns and berries and leaves. Queen Joan was sitting on a carved wooden throne in the middle on the room, her eyes closed and her body completely still. She had soft brown curls

underneath a crown made from twigs and flowers, and she was much older-looking than Queen Tania. She seemed like someone's nan, or a kindly older aunty – well, except that she was green.

She looked so peaceful, like she was sleeping. But I knew that only the spell would wake her, and that *I* was only one who could do it.

Omfra, Bran, Gillie and Max were all looking at me.

'I tried to memorise it,' I said, then narrowed my eyes in deep concentration and said, 'Oscar.'

'Huh?' said Bran. 'Who's Oscar?'

'My little brother.'

Bran was confused. 'And how can *he* help us?'

'Well,' I explained, 'it's true that he's usually not helpful when it comes to adventures. But this time, he might actually be useful.'

Bran looked more confused than ever. And so did the other pixies. Max too.

'My teacher,' I explained, 'at my old school, Mrs Lim, taught me a kind of poem where the first letters of each line spell a word – it's called an acrostic. And it just so happens that *this* one spells out my brother's name. Except,' I added nervously, 'in all the commotion at the fairy palace, and the complete panic of nearly being an apple and then a beetle, I'm not sure I can remember it exactly.'

'Try your best,' said Omfra gently. 'You've already done more than we can ever repay.'

So I tried.

On finishing this verse
So the freeze will thaw.
Come – break the curse
And move for evermore.
Re-animate

Then I stared at the queen, my mouth wide open. But she didn't move at all. I sighed and bowed my head. I mustn't have remembered it properly.

But Max gasped, and I looked up to see Queen Joan blink. She looked startled.

'Hooray!' said all the pixies, rushing to hug their queen – and hug us.

'Queen Joan,' said Bran, 'we're so pleased you're back.'

'Back?' she said.

'That nasty Queen Tania cast a spell to freeze you, so she could take over the whole forest.'

'Oh dear,' said Joan, her voice deep and soft. 'That is most unfortunate, Bran. But we mustn't call people names, should we?'

Bran shook his head sheepishly.

'We must forgive the fairies,' she continued.

'If one day we're going to live happily and peacefully alongside them, then we must set them an example.' She turned to us. 'So, who are you?' she asked. 'For pixies, you're not particularly green.'

'This is Alice,' said Omfra. 'And this is Max. They're humans – and *they're* the brave and clever ones who found the spell that unfroze you.'

Joan got up, shuffled over and shook us both warmly by the hand. 'Well, what excellent friends you two are, Alice and Max. I can't thank you enough.'

I did what I guessed was a curtsey, though I'd never done one before and I almost tripped myself up. 'You're welcome, Your Majesty.'

Max gave the queen a double thumbs-up.

Joan laughed. 'I have always thought that children are the best kind of humans.

Though you two are very small — even for children.'

'I shrunk them, Your Majesty,' said Omfra. To us, she added, 'And it's probably time to turn you back to your regular size.'

But Bran looked unusually sad. 'Can we please do it a bit later?' he said. 'I've something fun to show them.'

'Oh?' said Omfra.

'Berry-popping!' said Bran.

'Yes — can we?' said Gillie.

Omfra smiled. 'Of course,' she said. 'If it's okay with Max and Alice, that is.'

We both nodded enthusiastically. I had no idea what 'berry-popping' was, but it sounded brilliant.

Chapter Thirteen

Back outside the pixie house, and having changed back into our old clothes, we were waiting for Bran, who struggled over with a blackberry that was bigger than his head. 'Berry-popping,' he announced, 'is the best thing ever.'

He placed the berry on the ground and took a pine needle.

'These little round sacs of juice that make up the berry,' said Gillie, 'are called "drupelets". And when they're popped...'

Before Gillie could finish explaining, Bran, leaning over the berry with his mouth wide open, jabbed at it with the pine needle. A wave of dark red juice splashed up on to his face.

We all giggled. He licked his lips and wiped his face, then licked his hand.

'Delicious,' he said. 'And sticky. Sticky-licious! Your turn, Alice!' He handed me the pine needle.

I copied what he'd done – leant over the berry and poked it, hard. The juice splashed my face too – a gulpful into my mouth, and the rest on to my cheeks and neck and hair. It was cool and sweet and refreshing. Completely brilliant. Max had a turn, then the other two pixies, and then we all had another go, until there was nothing left to pop, and only the skin remained on the ground, like a burst water balloon.

Bran said, 'It's the best thing, right?'

'*So good*,' said Max.

Omfra smiled but then frowned. 'Alice and Max might get into trouble if they get home looking like that — all covered in juice.'

She was probably right. But Gillie had a plan. She led us to the trickling stream, which, because we were still small, came up to our tummies. We splashed and swam in the cool water, and the blackberry juice washed away.

After we'd climbed out, dripping wet, Omfra smiled. 'And if you go home drenched, you might get into even more trouble.'

This was true. But she waggled her wand and said, 'Time for a little spell, then. Come, warm breeze – dry these two with ease.'

A warm, powerful wind – like a hair-dryer – rushed over us, rippling our clothes and fluffing up our hair, and made us tingle all over.

'And now I suppose we'd better make you big again!' said Omfra.

I really didn't want the adventure to end, but I *was* missing my family, and getting hungry – all I'd had to eat and drink since my breakfast banana was Dana's tiny cupcake and some blackberry juice. So I nodded. Max seemed ready to go home too.

'Please come and see us again soon, though,' said Gillie.

'Oh, we will!' I said. 'I want you to tell me all about the forest, Gillie. See you soon, Bran – behave yourself! Take care, Omfra!'

Omfra gave me a big, squeezy hug and then she hugged Max too. 'Thank you both so much for what you did today,' she said. 'We pixies will be forever grateful.'

She pointed her wand at us –

we swirled and swirled and swooned – and then we were back in Max's garden, full-sized.

Max was grinning. 'So, are we adventure friends now, Alice?'

I laughed. 'Of course! And I'm sure those fairies will be causing trouble again soon. We'll probably have to go on another adventure to stop them.'

Max bounded up his garden back to the cottage, and at the back door turned to wave goodbye. I hurdled the fence and went back home too – exhausted.

Mum was in the kitchen chopping tomatoes when I walked in, and smiled when she saw me. 'Where have you been?'

'Oh, just on an adventure,' I replied casually.

Mum grinned.

'And I'll probably be going on lots more adventures, just so you know,' I added. 'With Max.'

'The boy next door?' she asked. I nodded. 'That was quick,' she said. 'Making a new friend.'

I smiled. I hadn't just made one friend – I'd made lots.

Later on, in my room, I was looking after Oscar. I was happy to be spending time with him (and super-grateful for his name!) but also a bit sad that all the excitement was over. When you've spent the morning doing magical things, baby-sitting is a bit – well – boring.

I noticed something caught in my hair, ran my fingers through it and found the tiny wooden tiara – it had fit me perfectly hours ago, but was now the size of a fingernail clipping. A souvenir! I was so amazed I failed to spot a cheeky baby toddling towards me, snatching the tiara out of my fingers and putting it to his mouth.

'Oscar, no!' I gasped. He paused, about to swallow the tiara. I grabbed his toy giraffe and held it out to him. 'Swap?' I said.

After a pause to consider my offer, he took the giraffe and handed me the tiara.

I studied it for a few moments, then popped it into the small treasure box I'd got for my last birthday. The wooden tiara was the first real treasure to go inside. I stared out of the window and tried to imagine what my next adventure with the pixies would be.

The fields out there certainly didn't look boring any more.

ALICE AND MAX'S ADVENTURES
WILL CONTINUE IN

PiXies
VS
FAiRiES

PONIES AND UNICORNS

COMING IN 2024 . . .